Bad Luck Brad

by Gail Herman
Illustrated by Stephanie Roth

The Kane Press
New York

To Norbert Dahlke, uncle extraordinaire
—S.R.

Book Design/Art Direction: Roberta Pressel

Copyright © 2002 by Kane Press, Inc.

Library of Congress Cataloging-in-Publication Data

Herman, Gail, 1959-
    Bad luck Brad / by Gail Herman ; illustrated by Stephanie Roth.
        p.   cm. — (Math matters.)
    Summary: On the last day of school Brad keeps running into bad luck, but by the end
of the day he realizes that there is always a chance things will get better.
    ISBN: 978-1-57565-112-5 (pbk. : alk. paper)
        [1. Luck—Fiction. 2. Chance—Fiction. 3. Probabilities—Fiction.] I. Roth, Stephanie, ill.
II. Title. III. Series.
    PZ7.H4315 Brad 2002
    [E]—dc21
2001038802
                                                                                CIP

eISBN 978-1-57565-566-6
                                                                        AC
10

First published in the United States of America in 2002 by Kane Press, Inc.
Printed at Worzalla Publishing, Stevens Point, WI, U.S.A., March 2016.

MATH MATTERS is a registered trademark of Kane Press, Inc.

Visit us online at **www.kanepress.com**

Like us on Facebook
facebook.com/kanepress

Follow us on Twitter
@kanepress

Chapter 1

BREAKFAST

Brad rubbed his eyes. He sat up in bed. Then he saw the clock: 7:45.

"Oh, no!" he cried. He had overslept— and on the last day of school. There was going to be a party, and everything!

Brad ran downstairs.

On the way, he bumped
into his sister, Lauren,
and his brother, Adam.

Then he tripped over a toy.
"Oh, man!" he muttered.

Brad got to the kitchen after everyone else.

"Looks like we all overslept," said Mr. Gold. "No eggs or pancakes this morning."

Mrs. Gold held out a bag of breakfast bars. "Everyone reach in and take one," she said.

The label on the bag read, "Lots of chocolate-chip bars! Lots of lemon-lime bars!" But Brad knew there weren't lots of chocolate-chip bars. He had eaten most of them.

"I want chocolate chip!" Adam said.

"Me, too!" said Lauren.

"So do I," said Brad.

Everyone reached.

"Not so fast!" said Mrs. Gold. She shook the bag. Lots of lemon-lime bars fell out— and only two chocolate-chip bars.

"Uh-oh," Brad thought. "Two chocolate-chip bars—and three kids." He crossed his fingers for luck.

"I want to be fair," Mrs. Gold said. She put the breakfast bars back into the bag. "You can each take out one bar. Lauren came into the kitchen first, so she'll go first. Then Adam, then Brad. No peeking!"

Lauren reached inside. "Ugh! Lemon-lime!" she said.

"My turn," said Adam. "Lucky me!" he yelled. "Chocolate-chip!"

"Now there's only one chocolate-chip bar left," Brad thought. He reached into the bag. "Unlucky me," he said. "Lemon-lime."

Brad sighed. He wanted the last day of school to be great. But already everything was going wrong.

✦ Chapter 2 ✦
SCHOOL

Mrs. Gold dropped Brad and his friend Pete at school. "I'll pick you up at the Candy Arcade," she said. "And then we'll do something special."

"Like a movie?" asked Brad.

"Like a movie," said his mom.

"Let's see *Space Flight 5!*" cried Brad.
"I loved *4, 3, 2,* and *1!*"

"No way!" said Pete. "I want to see
Dinosaur Days!"

"*Space Flight!*" said Brad as they handed in books.

"*Dinosaur Days!*" said Pete, as they cleaned out their desks.

"It's time for our party!" said Mrs. Costa. "Everyone put their grab-bag presents on the table."

"Yes!" cried Brad.

His present was an action figure—Commander Cody, hero of the Space Flight movies. He wanted it himself.

"I brought in T-Rex," Pete whispered.

"Cool," Brad said.

Brad wondered what the other presents
were. Paul's present was wrapped in
dinosaur paper. He could hear Zach say,
"I brought Commander Cody."

"Lots of great stuff," thought Brad.
"Maybe I'll be lucky."

Brad heard Lisa whisper to Ella. "I brought a Pony Parade pony. So did Annie and Abby and Sara."

"Humph," said Brad. He didn't want a silly pony. He didn't want any of the girl presents.

"Time for the grab bag!" said Mrs. Costa. "Just pick a name from this hat. Then go to the table and take the present with that name on it."

Everyone started lining up.

Brad looked at all the presents. Then it hit him. There were way more girls in the class than boys. So it was way more likely that he would pick a girl's name. "I'll probably wind up with a pony," he thought, "instead of something I *really* want."

It was Brad's turn. He pulled out a name—
Abby. "Oh no!" he thought. "I'm getting a
pony." He unwrapped the present anyway.

"You are *so* lucky!" squealed Sara. "You got
Pretty Pal the Palomino."

Lucky? Brad didn't feel lucky. He felt like
Bad Luck Brad.

Ella unwrapped her present. "Commander
Cody!" she said. "Just what I wanted!"

Brad sighed.

"Brad!" Lisa said. "I picked your name!
What did you bring?"

"Commander Cody," he said.

Lisa made a face.

"Hey!" Brad said. "Do you want to trade?"

"Sure!" said Lisa.

Just then the bell rang. School was over—
for the whole entire summer!

✦ Chapter 3 ✦
CANDY ARCADE

Brad and Pete raced to the Candy Arcade.
"I want a sour-peach T-Rex," Pete said.
"I want a gumball," Brad said. "A red one."

Brad looked at all the gumballs. The first machine had mostly white ones. The second had yellow and purple. The third machine had white, yellow, purple, green, black—and red, too!

Pete swallowed the last bit of his T-Rex. "I think I'll have a white gumball," he said. He put a quarter in the first machine. Out rolled a white gumball.

Brad dropped a quarter in the last machine. "Come on, red!" he shouted. *Plop!* Out came a white gumball.

Brad handed the gumball to Pete. "You're lucky. You got what you wanted—twice!"

Pete grinned. "That's because I try the machines that have a lot of what I like."

"I know," said Brad. "But none of the machines have lots of red. So I probably won't get a red gumball."

"You like purple gumballs, too," Pete said. "And this machine has plenty of purple!"

"I'll try it," said Brad. He put his last quarter in the slot. What came out? A yellow gumball.

Pete shook his head. "I guess it's never a sure thing. Here, I have another quarter."

"Maybe one more try," Brad thought.

Beep! Beep! It was Brad's mom.

"Too late now," said Pete. "Come on. Let's go see *Dinosaur Days*!"

"No," said Brad, "*Space Flight*!"

They ran to the car.

✦ Chapter 4 ✦
THE MOVIES

"Let's see when the movies are playing," said Mrs. Gold. "We need a 4:00 show."

She opened the newspaper. "*Space Flight* is playing in five theaters, and *Dinosaurs* in just one."

Brad grinned. There was a good chance the time would be right for *Space Flight*. It was playing in lots of theaters!

"*Dinosaurs* is playing at 5:15," said Mrs. Gold. "But *Space Flight* is playing at 3:30, 4:00, 4:30, 5:00, and 5:30."

"You said 4:00!" Brad shouted. "We get to see *Space Flight*!"

Pete groaned.

"I'm sorry," Brad told Pete. He knew just
how Pete was feeling. Then he remembered
something.

"Next time we can see *Dinosaur Days*," he said. "We'll have lots of chances. It's summer VACATION!"

PROBABILITY CHART

Sometimes "luck" depends on numbers!

One of these children will win the class art contest.

Tell why each sentence below is true.
- There is a **good chance** that a girl will win.
- There is a **good chance** that the winner will have brown eyes.

Suppose you close your eyes.
Then you pick a toy from each box.

Tell why you are **more likely** to pick a dinosaur from the red box than from the green box.